LADYBIRD BOOKS, INC.
Lewiston, Maine 04240 U.S.A.
© LADYBIRD BOOKS LTD MCMLXXXVII
Loughborough, Leicestershire, England

Printed in England

Chicken Licken

Adapted by DONNA R. PARNELL
Illustrated by JULIE DURRELL

Ladybird Books

One day,
an acorn fell on
Chicken Licken's head.

"Dear me," said Chicken Licken.
"The sky is falling!
I must tell the king."

So Chicken Licken
went down the road.

On the way,
Chicken Licken met Henny Penny.
''Where are you going?''
asked Henny Penny.

"The sky is falling,"
said Chicken Licken.
"I am going to tell the king."

"I will come with you,"
said Henny Penny.

So Chicken Licken and Henny Penny
went down the road.

On the way, they met Ducky Lucky.
"Where are you going?"
asked Ducky Lucky.

"The sky is falling,"
said Chicken Licken.
"We are going to tell the king."

"I will come with you,"
said Ducky Lucky.

So Chicken Licken, Henny Penny,
and Ducky Lucky went down the road.

On the way, they met Goosey Loosey.
"Where are you going?"
asked Goosey Loosey.

"The sky is falling,"
said Chicken Licken.
"We are going to tell the king."
"I will come with you,"
said Goosey Loosey.

So Chicken Licken, Henny Penny,
Ducky Lucky, and Goosey Loosey
went down the road.

This Way to PALACE→

On the way, they met Turkey Lurkey.
"Where are you going?"
asked Turkey Lurkey.

"The sky is falling,"
said Chicken Licken.
"We are going to tell the king."
"I will come with you,"
said Turkey Lurkey.

So Chicken Licken, Henny Penny,
Ducky Lucky, Goosey Loosey,
and Turkey Lurkey went down the road.

On the way, they met Foxy Loxy.
"Where are you going?"
asked Foxy Loxy.

"The sky is falling,"
said Chicken Licken.
"We are going to tell the king."

"I know the best way to
get there," said Foxy Loxy.
"You had better come with me."

So Chicken Licken, Henny Penny,
Ducky Lucky, Goosey Loosey,
and Turkey Lurkey
went with Foxy Loxy.

He led them right into his den.
Foxy Loxy's wife and babies
were waiting for their dinner.

The foxes gobbled up
Chicken Licken, Henny Penny,
Ducky Lucky, Goosey Loosey,
and Turkey Lurkey.

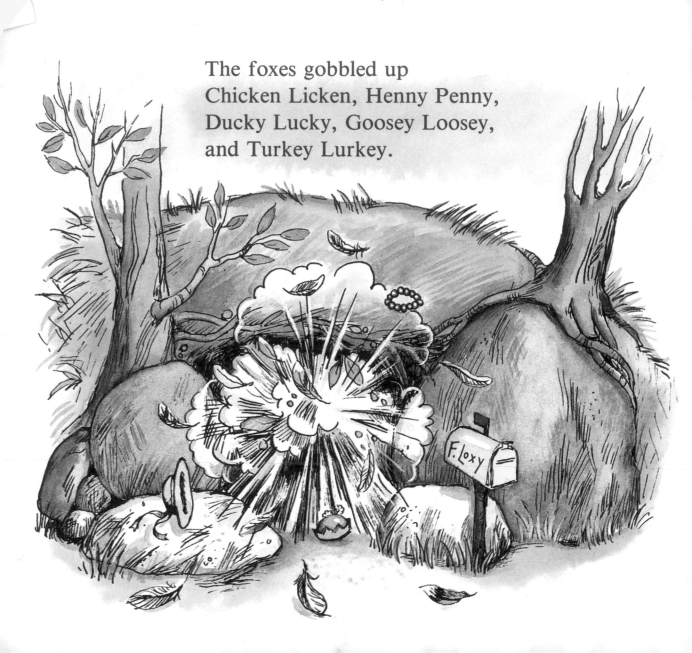

And Chicken Licken
never got to tell the king
that the sky was falling.